# A Treasury of Fairy Tales

ARCTURUS

ARCTURUS

This edition published in 2021 by Arcturus Publishing Limited
26/27 Bickels Yard, 151–153 Bermondsey Street,
London SE1 3HA

Copyright © Arcturus Holdings Limited

All rights reserved. No part of this publication may be reproduced, stored in a retrieval system, or transmitted, in any form or by any means, electronic, mechanical, photocopying, recording or otherwise, without prior written permission in accordance with the provisions of the Copyright Act 1956 (as amended). Any person or persons who do any unauthorized act in relation to this publication may be liable to criminal prosecution and civil claims for damages.

Author: Claire Philip
Illustrator: Helena Pérez García
Editor: Violet Peto
Designers: Amy McSimpson and Trudi Webb
Design Manager: Jessica Holliland
Managing Editor: Joe Harris

ISBN: 978-1-83857-464-2
CH007915NT
Supplier 29, Date 1220, Print run 9898

Printed in China

# Contents

Introduction ............................................. 4

Cinderella ............................................... 6

Puss in Boots ........................................... 22

Little Red Riding Hood ............................... 38

Snow White ............................................. 54

The Three Bears ....................................... 70

The Princess and the Pea ............................ 86

Aladdin ................................................ 102

Thumbelina ........................................... 118

About the Stories .................................... 134

Quick Quiz ........................................... 143

About the Illustrator and Author ................. 144

# Introduction

Storytelling has been an important part of people's lives since ancient times, when our ancestors gathered around the fire to laugh, gasp, and marvel at shared tales. The stories collected in this book are all more than a hundred years old, and some are much older than that. But they can still surprise, amuse, and entertain us now.

When these stories were first told, young people's lives were very different from those of children today. Some of these tales were originally warnings—about trusting strangers, or marrying the wrong person. Others were intended to be exciting or inspiring, and feature heroes and heroines overcoming the odds to live in a better world. After reading each story in the collection, you can find out about its origins by turning to the back of the book.

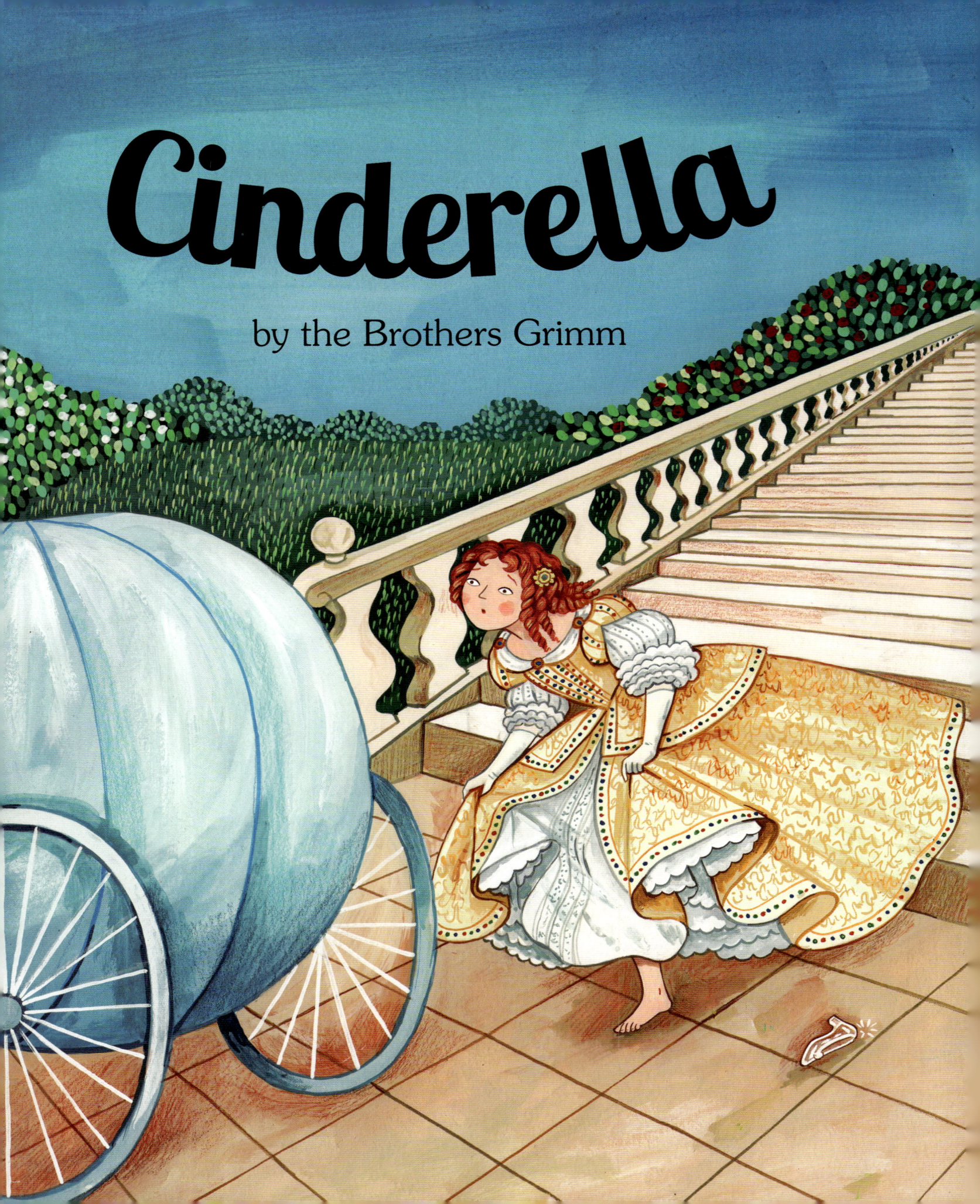

There once lived a gentleman who married a very proud, unkind woman. She was his second wife (his first had sadly passed away) and she had two daughters. Unfortunately, they were just as unpleasant as their mother.

The gentleman had one daughter already from his first marriage, and she was as sweet as could be. Her new stepmother was quite nice to her at first, but once she had moved into the gentleman's house, everything changed. She became incredibly disagreeable and gave her daughters the finest bedrooms in the house.

Cinderella

Meanwhile, the gentleman's daughter was made to sleep in the kitchen on a bed made of straw. Her stepmother told her it was now her job to clean the dishes, make the fires, and scrub the floors. The poor girl did as she was told. Each day she would wake early, carry out her chores, and then rest in the corner of the kitchen by the chimney. Her clothes soon became dirty from the cinders and the ashes from the fire, so her stepsisters nicknamed her "Cinderella."

Cinderella waited on her stepmother and stepsisters each day, slowly feeling sadder. One morning, as she was serving them breakfast, her stepmother opened a letter.

"It's from the palace!" she cried. "There is to be a ball for the prince, and everyone is invited."

"Wonderful!" said one of the stepsisters, named Gertrude.

"The prince is sure to see me and fall in love," gloated the other, who was called Nancy.

"Can I come?" said Cinderella. It was just what she needed to lift her spirits.

"No!" they all cried. "You'd be such an embarrassment!"

Cinderella

Poor Cinderella was so upset! She watched her stepsisters try on dress after dress over the coming weeks as they decided what to wear for the ball.

"Shall I wear my hair up with ribbons or down with a tiara?" Gertrude asked every morning.

"What do I care?" said Nancy as she repeatedly applied her make-up, each time putting on more and more lipstick.

The sisters talked of little else but the ball, each plotting ways to make the prince fall in love with them, so they could marry a royal.

On the day of the ball, Gertrude and Nancy began getting ready right after breakfast.

As they were doing their hair, they teased poor Cinderella, saying, "Don't you wish you were coming to the ball?"

"Why must you make fun of me?" said Cinderella, fighting back the tears.

Her stepsisters just laughed. "Imagine Cinderella arriving in her ash-covered clothes!" chortled Nancy.

"The prince would laugh in her face!" retorted Gertrude.

Soon after, a carriage arrived to take them to the ball. They clambered in, bickering over who the prince would like the most. Cinderella watched them leave, and as soon as they were out of sight, she let her tears fall. She was so sad.

"Why the tears, my darling?" someone said.

Cinderella looked up. Her godmother, who was a fairy, had arrived.

"I wish I could go to the ball," she cried.

"Well, we can fix that quite easily." Her fairy godmother smiled kindly, drawing her into a hug.

"R-really?" sniffed Cinderella.

"Yes, of course," said her fairy godmother. "We will need a pumpkin, though; fetch one from the vegetable patch!"

Confused but excited, Cinderella brought one over as quickly as she could. Her fairy godmother pulled out a magic wand from her midnight blue robes and struck the pumpkin sharply with it. Before Cinderella's eyes it grew—and grew—until it was the size of a carriage. Then, with a loud "POP," wheels, windows, and a door appeared! Cinderella looked inside. "Wow!" she cried. "It's just like a real carriage!"

"Now we need six mice and one rat!" said the fairy godmother.

Cinderella thought for a moment and then rushed into the cellar. There she found six little mice sleeping behind the firewood. Next, she ran to the stables and saw a rat sniffing around the drains. She took all the creatures to her fairy godmother, who once again took out her wand. Instantly the mice became six beautiful horses, and the rat became a coachman, who politely took a bow.

"Now, my dear," said the fairy godmother, "this time bring me six lizards."

Cinderella went to the pond and found the lizards lurking under some plant pots. She picked them up, one by one, and carried them back to her fairy godmother. With a flash of her wand, they became six dashing footmen who lined up behind the carriage, ready to go.

"But Godmother," Cinderella whispered, "I can't go in these rags."

The fairy godmother smiled her biggest smile yet and touched Cinderella's arm with her wand.

Her dirty clothes transformed into the most beautiful dress that Cinderella had ever seen. It was gold and silver and covered in gemstones. She was also wearing soft silk gloves and a string of pearls around her neck.

They glimmered beautifully in the moonlight.

"Look down at your feet," said the fairy godmother.

Cinderella did so and gasped.

"They are fairy shoes, my dear, made of glass," explained her godmother.

"Thank you," said Cinderella.

"You are very welcome. Now it is time for you to go to the ball," said the fairy godmother.

Cinderella climbed into her carriage and it began moving away, along the same road that her stepsisters had made their journey earlier that evening.

"There is just one thing," said the fairy godmother. "You must be home by midnight—that is when these spells end, and everything will return to normal."

Cinderella promised she would leave in plenty of time and waved good-bye.

When she arrived shortly after, she stepped down from the carriage and walked up the palace steps. The prince was standing in the doorway and was amazed at Cinderella's beauty and grace.

Cinderella

"Would you like to dance?" said the prince to Cinderella, who nodded happily.

Together they danced to the beautiful music all evening. At the end of each dance, he said to Cinderella, "Another?" and she said yes each time.

Her stepsisters were in the crowd watching with envy.

"He's so rude not to dance with us!" said Gertrude.

"I know," said Nancy. "Who is that anyway? In this light it looks a bit like … But no, it couldn't be."

Time passed so quickly that Cinderella couldn't believe her eyes when she looked up at the grand clock. It was nearly midnight! She thanked the prince for a wonderful evening and said that she must go to her carriage at once. Before the prince had a chance to say a thing, she dashed off—worried that the spell would end before she got home.

As Cinderella rushed to her carriage, she was in such a hurry that one of her glass shoes slipped from her feet and landed in the path.

Cinderella didn't want to see her stepsisters when they got home so she went straight to bed when she got back. The spell had ended, and her dress had changed back to her rags, as her fairy godmother had told her they would.

The next day, the girl at the ball was all the sisters could speak of. "She was stunning!" Nancy cried. "It was so unfair!"

Their mother added, "Now the prince is searching the land to find her and ask her to marry him! It's enough to make you sick!"

Later that day, the prince arrived at Cinderella's house in his search for the mysterious girl. Neither Gertrude nor Nancy's feet fit in the glass shoe when it was presented to them. But, before her stepmother could stop her, Cinderella stepped forward. And of course, the shoe fit perfectly. The prince cried with joy that he had found his bride.

"Outrageous!" cried Gertrude.

"Ridiculous!" shouted Nancy.

But the prince ignored them and proposed. Cinderella said yes, for she liked him very much, and together they returned to the palace, ready to plan a wedding!

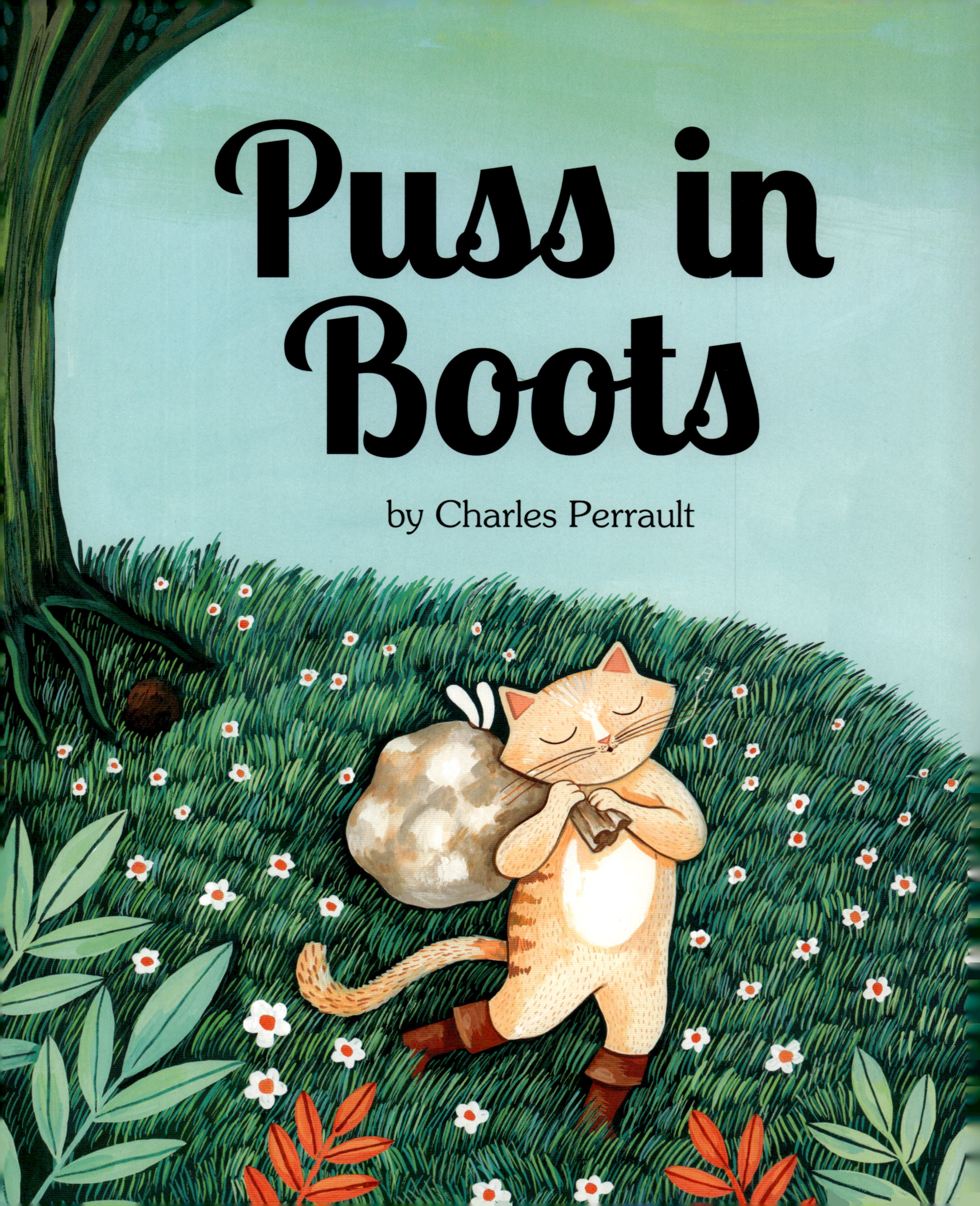

Puss in Boots

**O**nce there lived a very poor man whose only possession was his ginger cat named Puss. The impoverished man had the clothes on his back and a few coins in his pockets—that was all. The man wasn't happy living this way. He saw his friends living in nice houses and buying fancy clothes, and he decided enough was enough. There was no reason why he couldn't come up with a way to make his fortune.

When the man sat down and pondered ways to become rich, it turned out that he had very few ideas.

"This might be more difficult than I thought," he said to Puss, who was lying nearby in the sun. "I have nothing to sell, no instrument to play, and no talents to show to the world."

The man was really quite forlorn until his cat, who happened to be able to speak, exclaimed, "Master! Do not worry. If you find me some boots, we will make a fortune fast!"

"Boots!" cried the man with laughter. "Why would you want boots?"

"To wear, of course!" said the cat. "No-one will have seen anything like it. People will come from far and wide to see us—and pay good money too!"

"Interesting," said the man as he stroked his chin.

"I'll dazzle everyone," said Puss, "even the king! Just find me the boots. Oh—and I'll need a bag too—then we can get to work."

At the mention of the king, the man became very excited. "I'll get them right now!" he exclaimed.

The man hurried quickly to the market and with his last few coins, he bought a pair of brown leather boots and a large bag. He whistled joyfully as he walked back to his cat, who had been waiting for him.

"Here you go," said the man. "Just as you asked."

"Excellent," said Puss as he stepped into the boots. He could now walk upright.

The man could hardly believe his eyes! "Wow! Puss!" he said. "You really will be the talk of the town!

Puss smiled and began walking with a strut.

The next day, Puss set out early in the morning to a nearby field. He huddled down in the long grass waiting patiently next to a rabbit warren. He had placed the bag over its entrance. Inside the bag was some stale bread that his master had decided was too tough to eat.

After about half an hour, Puss heard movement. Two rabbits hopped out of their home and, one after the other, walked into the bag.

"Got them!" said Puss. "These will make a great gift for the king!"

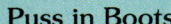

Puss ordered the rabbits to be sent to the king with a message saying that they were a present from the "Marquis of Carabas." The poor man asked why Puss wasn't telling the truth and he replied soothingly, "Wait and see—soon the king will be ready to reward us. First, however, we have to impress him."

The poor man wasn't sure, but he had no choice but to listen to the cat, who informed him that he was setting out to hunt again—this time for some juicy partridges.

When the king was told that the Marquis of Carabas had sent more delicious gifts to him, he began wondering who this generous man was. "I should like to meet him," said the king.

Later that day, the king decided he wished to take a trip in his carriage around the countryside. Puss had been keeping a close eye on the palace, and so when the king left, he ran ahead to the cornfields and called to the farmers, "When the king asks who owns these farms, say that they belong to the Marquis of Carabas!"

The farmers were so surprised to hear a cat wearing boots speak that they agreed on the spot! When the king leaned out of his carriage to ask who owned the fields, he was surprised to hear the name yet again.

"This Marquis of Carabas must be really quite something," he said to his daughter, the princess, who was sitting alongside him. "I think I shall invite him to come to the palace."

"Good idea," said the princess thoughtfully. "His people seem to admire him very much."

Suddenly, the king spotted someone in the road and ordered the carriage to be stopped.

He climbed down and came face to face with a soaking wet man in his underclothes—and Puss in his boots.

"What happened here?" asked the king.

"My master," spoke Puss as he pointed at the poor man, "was robbed of his carriage and clothes and pushed into the river by thieves!"

The king, shocked by the tale and the talking cat—said "Who is your master?"

"The Marquis of Carabas!" said Puss.

The king could hardly believe his ears! "The Marquis of Carabas, are you sure?"

"Yes, your majesty! This is he!" said Puss. "Would you be so kind as to let him take shelter in your carriage?"

"Of course!" cried the king.

"I shall run ahead to our castle, my king, and order a grand feast to be served—will you join us?"

"Certainly!" said the king.

And so the poor man clambered up into the royal carriage and sat opposite the princess, who smiled very kindly at him.

Puss in Boots was delighted! The plan was working just as he had imagined. He ran as fast as he could through the countryside, telling everyone he saw that when the king passed through, they must say that everything in sight is owned by the Marquis of Carabas.

"We had better do as the talking cat says," they said to each other. "Who knows what he is capable of!"

And so each time the king paused the carriage, he was told that the man next to him was the owner of the land.

Now, Puss had come to the most dangerous point in his plan. The castle that he was leading the king to actually belonged to an ogre, known for being mean-spirited, especially to cats.

He was also said to have the power to change into any animal at will. When Puss arrived at the castle, he asked at once to see the ogre, claiming he had important news.

As Puss entered the hall, the ogre looked up, surprised to see a cat in boots. "What do you want?" he shouted.

"Someone is about to attack your castle," said Puss. "If you do something for me, I shall tell you how to win the battle."

The ogre thought for a minute. "What do you want?" he said.

"I have heard that you can turn into any animal," replied Puss. "I wish to see it."

"That's easy," said the ogre. "What creature shall I become?"

"A mouse," said Puss calmly.

"Fine," said the ogre. "And when I win you shall become my pet!"

The ogre turned into a mouse, but before he could change back, Puss pounced and swallowed him up!

Puss in Boots

"Cats will be cats!" Puss chuckled as he licked his lips and cleaned his whiskers.

"The king's carriage is coming through the gates," Puss heard a servant call.

He ran out and shouted, "I have defeated the ogre! You are now servants of the Marquis of Carabas!"

Everyone in the castle was so overjoyed that the terrible ogre was gone that they agreed at once.

"Prepare a grand feast for the king," ordered Puss. "Only the finest food and drink will do—and remember, this is the Marquis of Carabas' castle!"

And so when the king, princess, and the poor man pulled up at the castle, they were met by a proud-looking Puss and a host of servants.

Later, as they sat eating a feast, the king exclaimed, "My daughter has taken a liking to you, Marquis. It would be a blessing to have such a great man in the family. If you will agree, she would like you to be her husband."

And that is how a poor man, with the help of a cat, came to own a grand fortune and married into royalty.

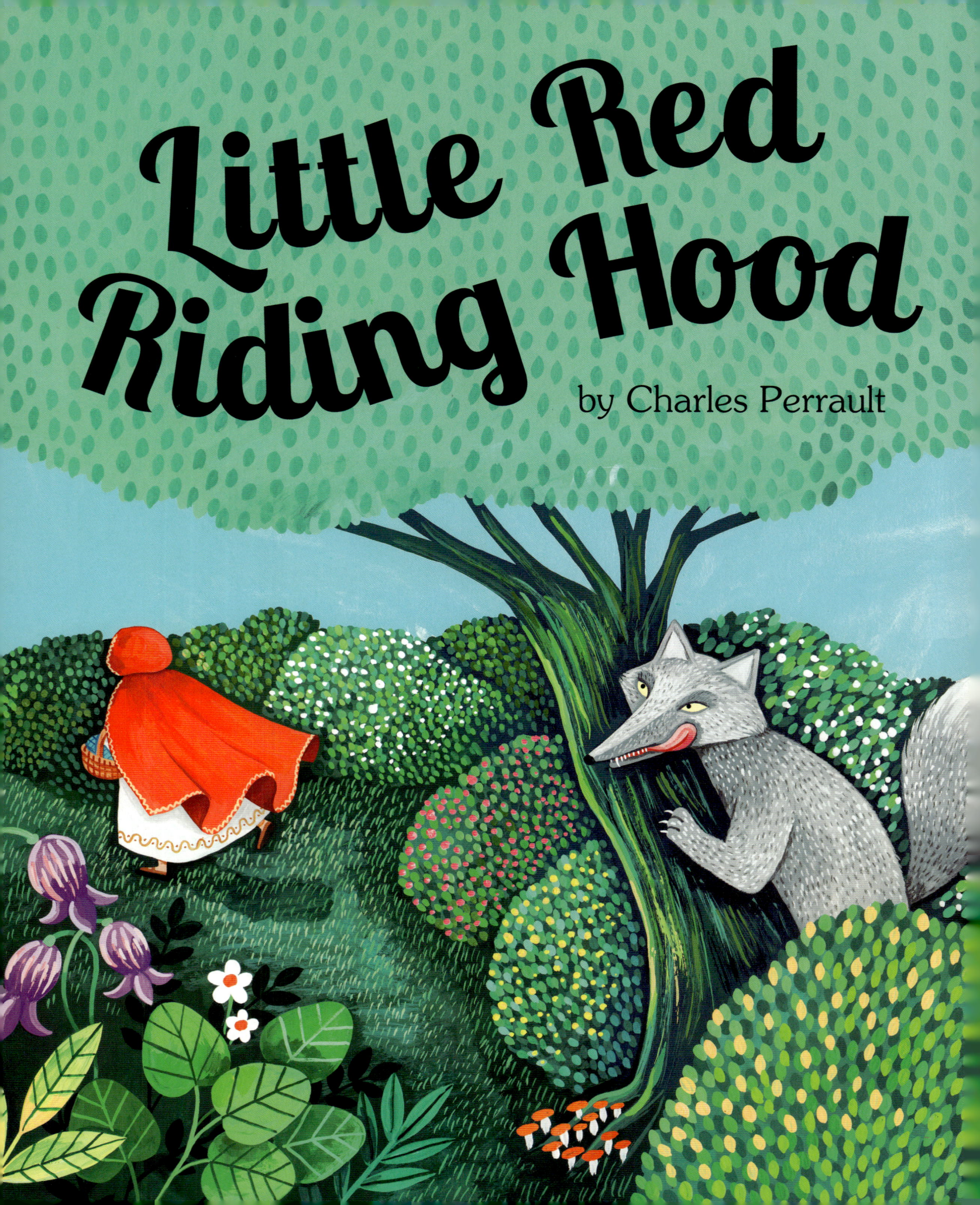

# Little Red Riding Hood

by Charles Perrault

# Little Red Riding Hood

There was once a little girl who lived in a beautiful, rose-covered cottage at the edge of a pretty village. The girl always wore a bright red cloak, so people called her Little Red Riding Hood. Her old grandmother, who she loved very much, lived on the other side of the large woods nearby, and was getting too old to travel. Very often, the little girl would walk through the woods to visit her grandmother and take her meals.

Early one morning, Little Red Riding Hood's mother asked her to take her grandmother a basket of eggs, bread and butter, and a cake.

Little Red Riding Hood

"Poor Grandma isn't feeling very well," her mother said. "Please can you take this food to her? I'm just too busy and you always cheer her up!"

"Yes, of course," said Little Red Riding Hood. She loved walking down the winding trails and looking at all the different wildflowers and mushrooms that grew along the edges. And she loved spending time with her grandmother.

"Just make sure you stick to the path," her father said. "And don't talk to any strangers."

"I know, Father!" giggled Little Red Riding Hood. "Don't worry!" And off she skipped with the basket in her arms.

Once she was in the woods, Little Red Riding Hood felt happy and excited—the weather was bright and sunny and there wasn't a cloud in the sky. As she danced happily along the path, she noticed that the wildflowers were looking very pretty that day.

"I'll pick some for Grandma!" she said out loud to herself, and she collected a bunch of cowslips, poppies, and cornflowers.

What Little Red Riding Hood didn't know, was that something was watching her from a distance. Slinking from tree to tree, a great big wolf was tracking her. It was very hungry and thought that Little Red Riding Hood might make a very good meal indeed.

Little Red Riding Hood had no idea she was in danger. Walking happily along, she spotted a fairy mushroom ring just off the path. She thought about her father's warning and said out loud to herself, "I'll just have a quick look at it to see if the fairies left anything behind."

Little Red Riding Hood walked up to the mushrooms and crouched down.

"I wonder where all the fairies are now?" she said dreamily.

"Wouldn't you like to know?" said a loud, gruff voice. Poor Little Red Riding Hood jumped out of her skin!

"Oh don't worry, dear, I shan't harm you," the wolf said, sneakily.

"Who—Who are you?" Little Red Riding Hood whispered.

"I'm Mr. Wolf," said the wolf. "And you are Little Red Riding Hood. I've seen you before. Tell me, what have you got there in your basket?"

"Just some food, Mr. Wolf, and some flowers for my grandma," said Little Red Riding Hood. She was feeling very eager to get away.

"Very nice," said the wolf slowly, licking his lips. "And where does your grandmother live, Little Red Riding Hood?"

"She lives along this path and all the way out the other side of the woods, Mr. Wolf," she replied.

"Excellent," said the wolf rather menacingly. "Well, have a pleasant morning, Little Red Riding Hood. Good-day."

As the wolf slunk away, poor Little Red Riding Hood dashed back onto the path, wishing she had listened to her father's warning. She paused for a moment and then walked toward her grandmother's a little more quickly than before.

Meanwhile, the wolf had run ahead. He had darted through the woods as quickly as he could till he found Grandma's cottage.

He walked up the path and rapped sharply on the door.

"Who is there?" called the old lady. "Little Red Riding Hood, is that you?"

"Yes, Grandma, it is me!" said the wicked wolf.

"You sound very husky, my dear!" said Grandma, a little suspiciously. "Come in … "

And so the wolf pushed open the door.

Poor Grandma was so frightened to see the wolf instead of her granddaughter!

"Leave me alone!" she cried as she jumped inside her wardrobe, shutting the door tightly behind her.

The wolf laughed and began walking toward her, ready to fling open the wardrobe door, when he heard singing … Little Red Riding Hood was almost here.

"Two meals then!" he snarled. He stopped where he was and picked up Grandma's nightcap, which had fallen from her head. He put it on and climbed under the bedclothes.

"Little Red Riding Hood will be here any second," he said with a snarl. "What a surprise she is about to get!"

The wolf didn't have to wait long.

"Hello, Grandma!" Little Red Riding Hood called as she opened the door. "It's me! I have food for you from Mother and some flowers from the woods!"

Little Red Riding Hood walked to the kitchen and put down the basket. She walked happily toward her grandmother's bedroom—then paused. Something was wrong …

"Why, what big ears you have, Grandma." Little Red Riding Hood said nervously.

"All the better to hear you with, my dear," said the wolf.

"And Grandma," she spoke again, "what large eyes you have."

"All the better to see you with, my dear," said the wolf. Little Red Riding Hood was getting very frightened now.

"Grandma, what a large nose you have!"

"Yes, my dear," said the wolf, now licking his lips, "all the better to smell you with!"

Little Red Riding Hood was looking around the room for her real grandma, but couldn't see her anywhere.

"And what a big mouth you have," she gulped fearfully.

"Yessss! Little Red Riding Hood!" said the wolf. "All the better to EAT you with!"

As he spoke, the wolf sprung out from the bed toward the little girl, who shrieked!

She jumped back just in time, as the wolf took a swipe at her. Little Red Riding Hood ran around the house, the wolf hot on her heels. She knocked over a chair to try and stop the wolf from getting to her, and she even threw a candlestick at him.

Little Red Riding Hood

"Sorry Grandma!" she called as she flung ornament after ornament behind her, each one bouncing off the wolf's head and buying her a few seconds.

"Give up little girl," said the wolf. "I'm going to catch you!"

"Oh no you won't," cried Grandma as she burst out of the wardrobe.

"Grandma!" cried Little Red Riding Hood.

"No wolf is going to eat my granddaughter!" she roared. The tussle continued. For an old lady, Little Red Riding Hood's grandmother was quick! She picked up her broom and charged towards the wolf, who was taken by surprise.

Little Red Riding Hood

Little Red Riding Hood dashed to the kitchen and grabbed her basket. One by one, she pelted the wolf with the eggs she had brought, all while shouting, "Help!" at the top of her lungs.

The wolf was worried. "What's this!" he thought. "The old lady and the little girl are winning!"

Now, Little Red Riding Hood's father had had a strange feeling that morning when his daughter set off. After he had finished his breakfast he began chopping wood, but he couldn't shift the feeling that something was wrong.

Half an hour after Little Red Riding Hood left for Grandma's, her father had followed along the same path. And thank goodness he did! Just as Little Red Riding Hood threw her last egg at the wolf, her father burst through the door wielding an axe.

The wolf took one look at the large man, through the egg whites, and jumped out an open window. Little Red Riding Hood's father dashed out after him, and returned later saying that there would be no more trouble from the wolf.

"Grandma was amazing," Little Red Riding Hood said to her father.

Grandma had fallen asleep in her chair.

"It doesn't surprise me," he said with a grin, "though I thought she was unwell!"

And together, before heading home, they shared some of the cake Little Red Riding Hood had brought with her.

# Snow White

by the Brothers Grimm

Snow White

A long time ago, in the middle of a cold winter, a queen sat in her palace bedroom near a window. She was sewing a blanket for the baby she was expecting, while watching snowflakes fall outside. The queen was so focused on the storm that she pricked her finger and a drop of blood landed on the white material. She thought that the red and white looked very striking together, so when her baby girl was born with skin as white as snow and cheeks as red as blood, she called her "Snow White."

Snow White

Now, very sadly, the poor queen passed away soon after Snow White was born. About one year later, the king remarried so that the baby would have someone to help look after her. His new wife was also beautiful, with a sweet voice and refined manners.

However, she had an air of pride about her that the servants of the palace disliked immediately. They wondered why she spent so much time each day looking at her reflection in a grand mirror, which she kept in her dressing room.

One morning, the servants decided to find out why the mirror was so special. They tiptoed to the new queen's dressing room and waited for just a few short minutes. Then they overheard her say in a soft, cooing voice: "Mirror, mirror on the wall, who is the fairest of us all?"

And to their surprise, it replied: "You, my queen, are the fairest of them all."

The new queen looked very happy indeed with this answer—for the mirror could only tell the truth. Whatever question it was asked, the answer it gave was correct.

Now, as Snow White grew up, it became more and more clear that she was a very pretty girl. And one day, when she was eighteen years old, the mirror gave the queen a different answer when she asked: "Mirror, mirror on the wall, who is the fairest of us all?"

The queen was furious to hear, "The queen was fairest yesterday, but Snow White is now the fairest—or so they say."

The queen felt so much envy bubble up inside her that she nearly broke the mirror! She was furious that Snow White was more beautiful than her, and she began concocting an evil plot to get rid of her! She sought out a huntsman and ordered him to take Snow White deep into the forest and make sure the girl could never come back.

Snow White

The huntsman took Snow White to the heart of the woods, but he couldn't bring himself to harm her.

"Snow White," he cried, "you must run away! The queen wants you dead!"

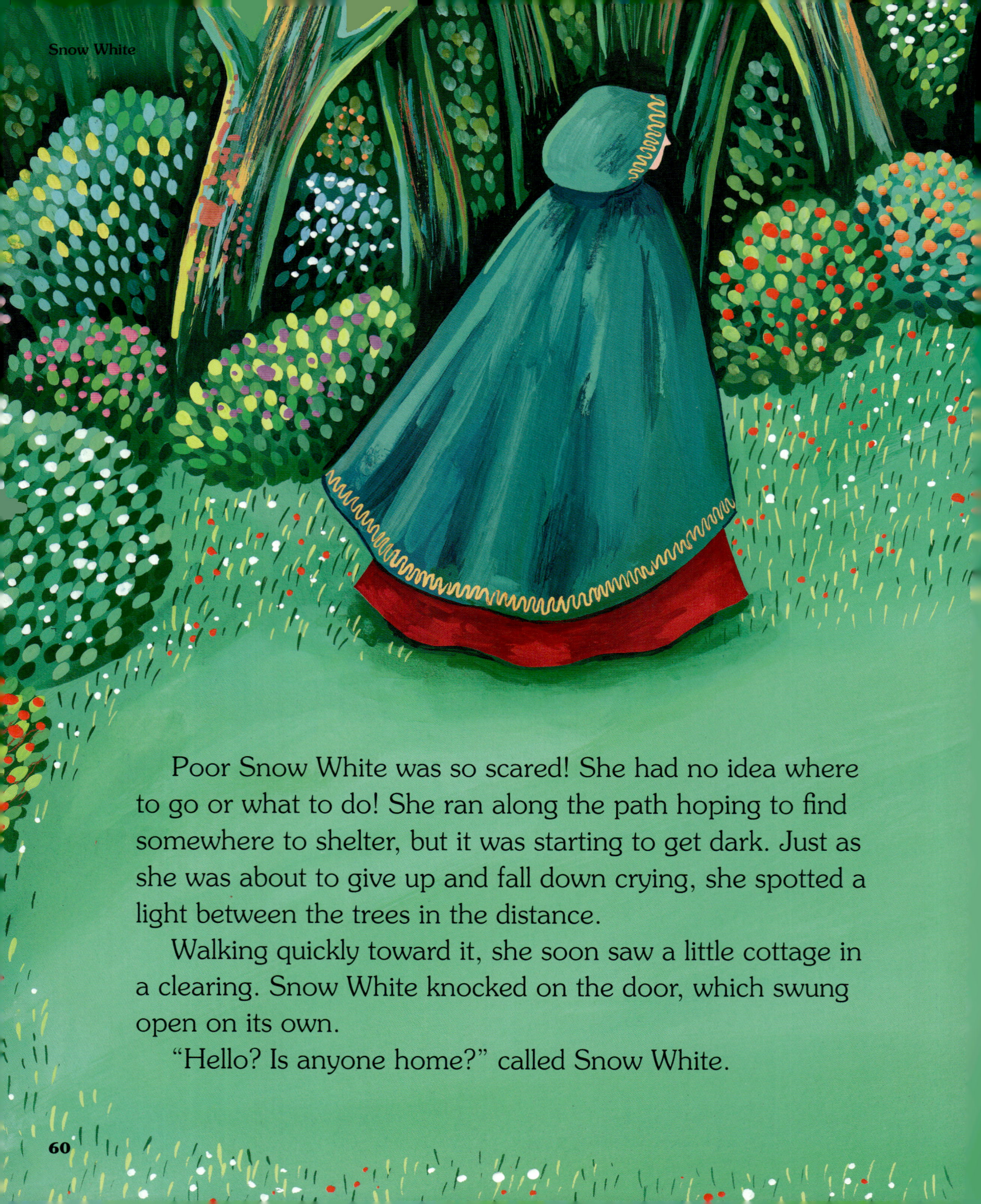

Poor Snow White was so scared! She had no idea where to go or what to do! She ran along the path hoping to find somewhere to shelter, but it was starting to get dark. Just as she was about to give up and fall down crying, she spotted a light between the trees in the distance.

Walking quickly toward it, she soon saw a little cottage in a clearing. Snow White knocked on the door, which swung open on its own.

"Hello? Is anyone home?" called Snow White.

But there was no answer. She took a few steps inside the door and looked around. Everything was very small and neat. She saw a table, and on it were seven plates, seven spoons, and seven cups.

"Where is everyone?" she said aloud as she walked into the next room.

She found herself in a bedroom with seven small beds arranged in a row! Each had a blanket with a different pattern on it.

Snow White

Snow White was very hungry and thirsty indeed, so she went back into the kitchen. She took a very small amount from each of the seven plates and took one small sip from each cup—she didn't want to take someone's whole meal.

After that, she felt so tired that she slipped under the blankets on one of the beds, thinking that she would just rest for a few moments and leave before whoever lived in the cottage came home. Instead, she fell into a very deep sleep—poor Snow White was exhausted.

Snow White

And so, when the owners of the cottage—seven dwarfs—came home, they had quite a surprise! They had been out in the mountains digging for silver and gold and were ready for their supper.

One of the dwarfs picked up his cup and said, "Someone has had a sip of my drink!"

"Who could that be?" said another.

A third, who had gone into the bedroom said, "There's a girl here asleep in my bed!"

The dwarfs crowded around Snow White and gently woke her. "Don't be scared now, but who are you?"

63

Snow White sat up in the bed and told them what had happened—how her stepmother, the queen, had banished her to the forest, knowing how dangerous it was, and ordered her never to return.

"The brute!" said one of the dwarfs.

"Well," said another, "will you stay here and look after our house for us? It takes a lot of work to keep the house clean and our bellies full—you'd be a great help."

Snow White was delighted—she agreed at once to stay with the friendly dwarfs, who made up a new bed for her right away.

So, each morning the dwarfs went off into the mountains to search for silver and gold, and Snow White took care of the house and prepared their evening meal.

In the meantime, back at the palace, the queen's mirror had told her that Snow White was still the fairest, and that she was being protected by the dwarfs in the forest.

"I will have to go and get rid of her myself!" shouted the queen when she heard the news.

The next day the queen disguised herself as an old woman and entered the forest. When she reached the cottage, she knocked on the window and when Snow White opened it, the queen handed her a crisp apple, which she had poisoned.

"Thank you," said Snow White, and she took a bite. Immediately the poor girl fell to the ground. The queen dashed off laughing to herself. "I am rid of her at last," she cackled.

When the dwarfs got home that evening they were beside themselves. They placed her in a glass coffin and wept.

The strange thing was that although Snow White would not wake, she looked very much alive. Each day the dwarfs would visit her and hope that maybe she could come back to life. They had all but given up hope when one morning a prince from a nearby kingdom rode past. As he climbed down from his horse to take a closer look, his horse knocked the coffin.

This made the piece of apple in Snow White's mouth fall out! She opened her eyes at once. The dwarfs opened the coffin and laughed and hugged with joy!

The prince thought that Snow White was the most beautiful girl he had ever seen, and he invited her to spend the rest of the day with him at his palace. He hoped that she would fall in love with him, as he had with her.

Snow White accepted, and they spent a happy afternoon together walking around the palace gardens. Captivated by his kindness and charm, Snow White soon fell in love with the prince, just as he had hoped she would.

A few months later a grand wedding took place, and all the dwarfs attended.

When the queen found out that Snow White was not only alive but married to a handsome prince, she rushed to her mirror.

"Mirror, mirror on the wall, who is the fairest of us all?" the queen shouted at the top of her lungs.

The mirror slowly replied: "The queen was fairest yesterday—but now it's the prince's bride they say."

The queen went bright red with fury and envy. She was so cross that she packed her bags and left the palace immediately, never to be seen again!

Meanwhile, Snow White was very happy with the prince in her new home, and she always made time to visit her old friends in the forest.

# The Three Bears

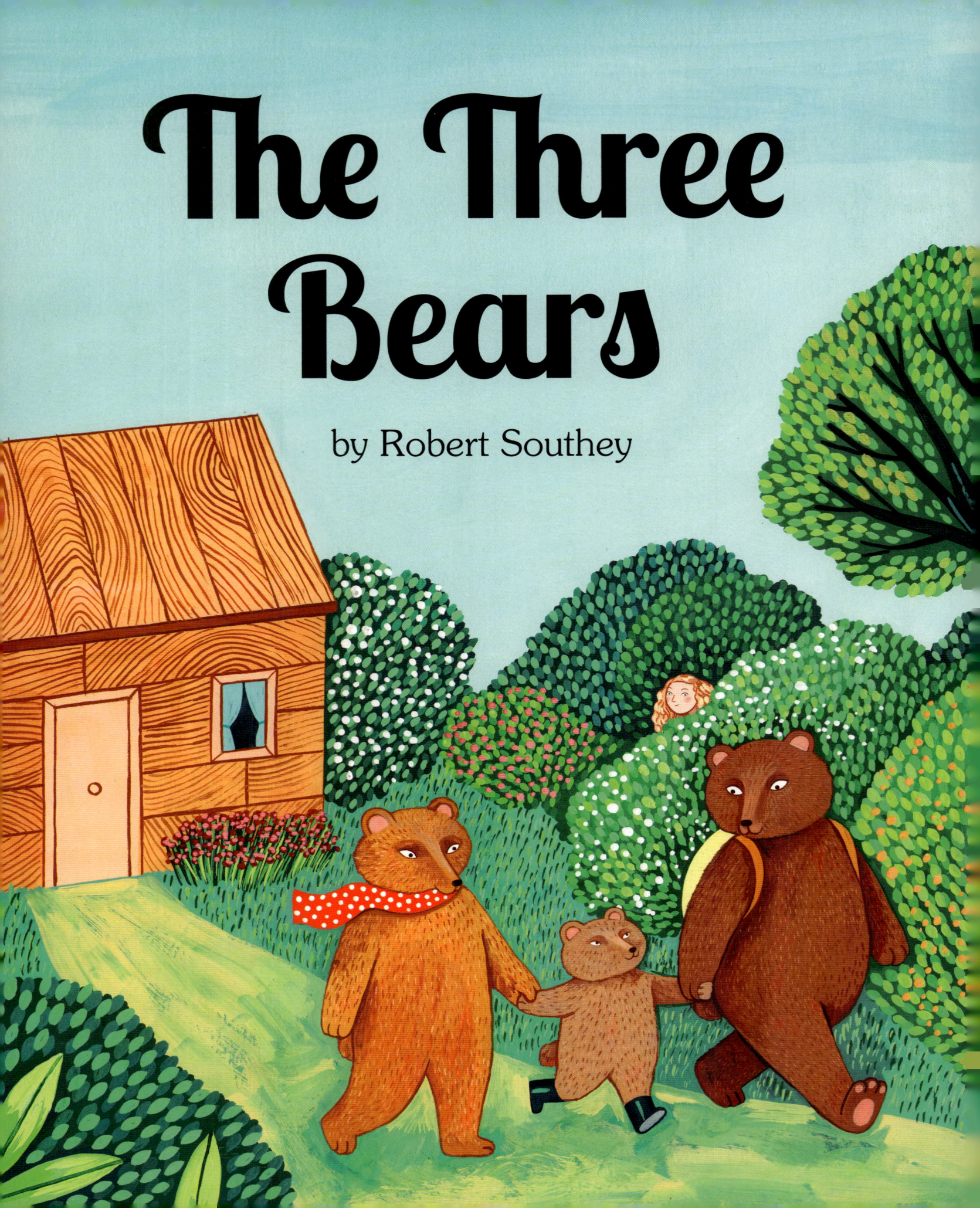

by Robert Southey

The Three Bears

Long ago, a family of brown grizzly bears lived in a big wood far from anyone—they weren't very sociable, you see. The biggest bear, Mr. Bear, was huge and quite grumpy most of the time (because he was often hungry). Mrs. Bear was a bit smaller and had a much sweeter temper. The littlest bear, their only cub, was very playful and kind.

Together, the three bears lived in a cottage enjoying each other's company and minding their own business.

Now these bears were very particular about their belongings. Mr. Bear had a great big granite bowl that he liked to eat his porridge from each morning while sitting in his special big chair. Mrs. Bear liked to eat her breakfast from a large mixing bowl while sitting in her medium-sized wooden chair. Baby Bear had a small wooden bowl and preferred to sit in a nice wicker chair.

One morning, as the bears were sitting down to breakfast, Mr. Bear had an idea to go fishing while their steaming porridge cooled down. There was a spot by the river that was just excellent for salmon catching, and the sun was shining brightly.

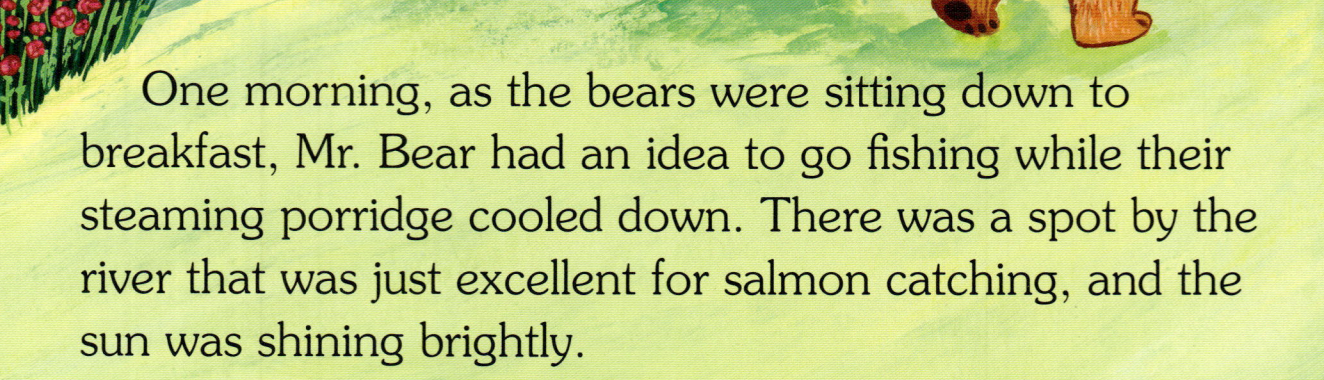

The Three Bears

"It's a great day for it; what do you think my dear?" he asked Mrs. Bear.

"It sounds wonderful," said Mrs. Bear.

Mr. Bear smiled and sharpened his claws so he was ready to swipe at the fish.

The Three Bears

Now, the bears would always leave their front door unlocked when they went out. There was no one nearby—or so they thought. But that morning, a girl from the village on the other side of the mountain walked close to the house and saw the family leaving.

"Bears wearing clothes!" she said. "This I have to see!"

And she snuck closer to get a better look. The girl was called Goldilocks on account of her golden curls. She watched the bears walk down the path toward the river for a short time—then crept back to the house to look inside.

When Goldilocks got to the cottage, she looked over her shoulder to check that the coast was clear, then pushed open the door and stepped inside. She went into the kitchen and on the table was a great big stone bowl. Goldilocks peered into it and saw porridge. Picking up the bowl, she had a small taste.

"Yuck!" she cried. "Too salty!"

Next she went to the mixing bowl.

"Ouch! Too hot!" she howled, dropping the bowl on the floor in shock.

I'll try this third bowl," said Goldilocks as she picked up Baby Bear's breakfast. "Mmm," she sighed, "just right!" And she ate it all up.

After that, she went to sit down on the wicker chair next to her. However, as she dropped her weight onto it, it broke!

The Three Bears

"Oh no!" she cried. "The bears will be so angry!" Goldilocks was scared. She looked for something to fix the chair and clean up the mess, but she soon gave up.

"As long as I leave before they get home, it's no matter," she said, quite selfishly, before taking a look around the rest of the house.

As she walked through the rooms she picked up whatever she wanted, not minding at all that nothing there belonged to her. When she came to the bedroom, she thought to herself that she really was quite tired after all the walking around she had done; perhaps she could rest her head.

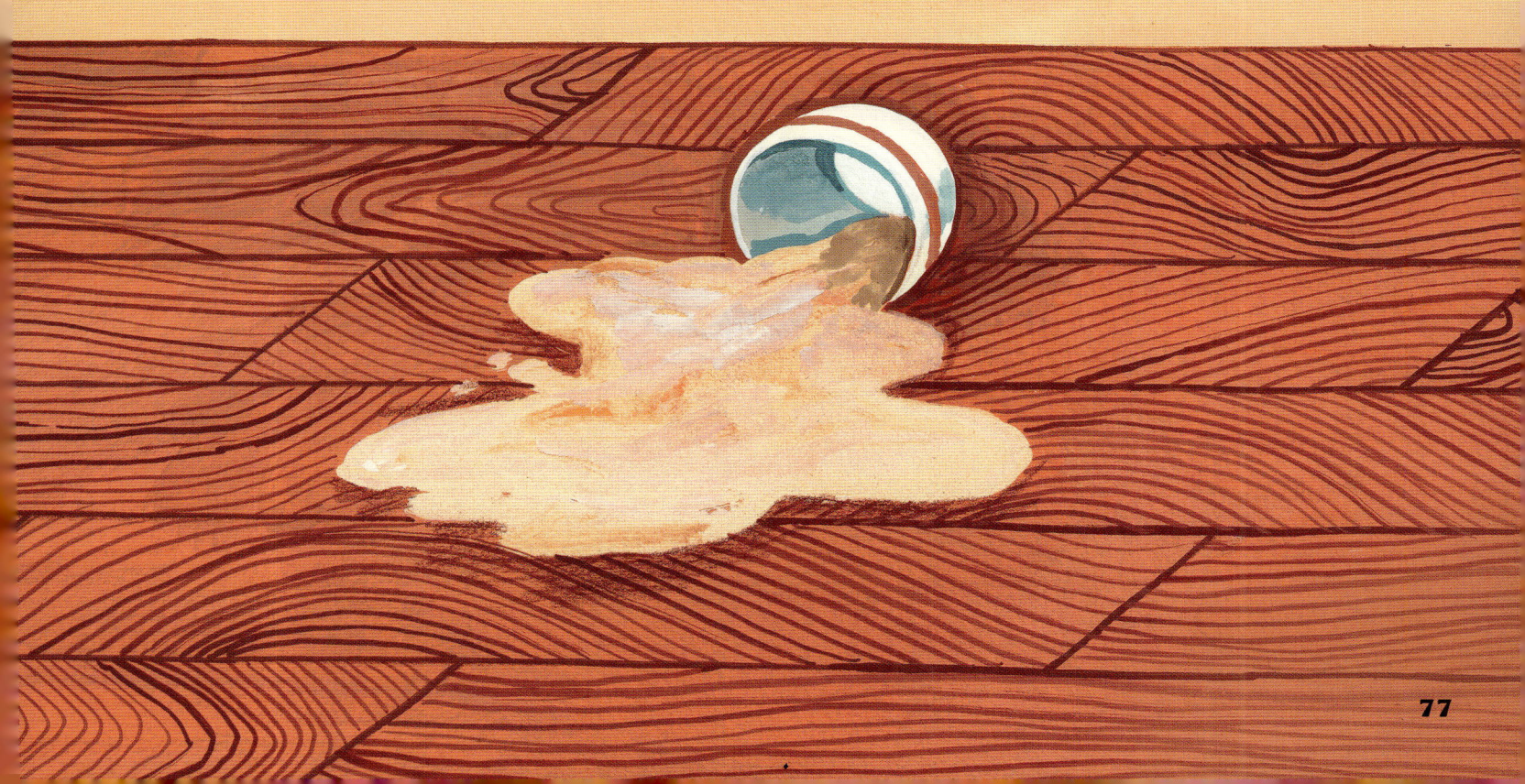

The Three Bears

Goldilocks tried the first bed she came to. It was Mr. Bear's. She climbed in and lay down but very quickly jumped back out again—the mattress was so hard.

"I'll never get to sleep on that!" she said.

Goldilocks walked around to the next bed, Mrs. Bear's. The mattress was softer but the pillow made her feel like her head was on a pile of bricks.

"So uncomfortable!" she cried.

With only one choice left, she walked over to Baby Bear's bed.

The Three Bears

"Oh this is just right!" she sighed, pulling the covers around her shoulders.

Goldilocks quickly fell into a deep sleep—so deep that she didn't hear the bears when they arrived back home.

Already in a bad mood after an unsuccessful fishing trip, Mr. Bear was FURIOUS when he saw that the front door was ajar.

"Someone's been in our house!" he yelled. "Can you believe it!"

The Three Bears

He dropped his knapsack down on the ground and stormed around to see if anything had been taken. He soon saw that everything was still there, but lots of things had been moved around.

"They must have gone," said Baby Bear.

"Let's eat," said Mrs. Bear, "before our porridge gets cold."

Mr. Bear took one look at his bowl and saw that it wasn't as full as when he had left it.

"The thief has eaten some of my porridge!" he bellowed.

Mrs. Bear looked at her bowl, "Oh my goodness!" she said. "Someone has spilled mine on the floor!"

Poor Baby Bear burst into tears. "Someone has eaten ALL of my porridge—there's none left at all!"

"Who would do such a strange thing?" said Mrs. Bear as she picked up her cub to comfort him.

"I'll make you some more soon," she said kissing his forehead. "Why don't we sit down and read a story?"

The Three Bears

Baby Bear liked that idea, but then he saw his crumpled chair on the floor and gave another great wail. "My chair is broken!" he cried.

"What if whoever ate our porridge and sat in our chairs is still here?" said Mrs. Bear.

"If they are, I'll find them!" growled Mr. Bear. "I'm going to look in the bedroom."

He stepped as lightly as a large bear could until he reached the bedroom. Mrs. Bear and Baby Bear followed quietly.

They crept into the room and saw that the bedclothes on Mr. and Mrs. Bear's beds had been moved. And there, in Baby Bear's bed—was Goldilocks!

Goldilocks gave a loud snort in her sleep, waking herself up. She rubbed her eyes, yawning sleepily—and then jumped out of her skin! The three bears roared as loudly as they could.

"Who are you?" growled Mrs. Bear. "And what are you doing in our house?"

**The Three Bears**

Goldilocks looked uncomfortable. "I was lost," she lied, "and needed help!"

"I don't believe you!" said Mr. Bear who could spot a fib a mile off. "You are a thief!"

Goldilocks leapt out of bed and made a dash for the door, but Mr. Bear was hot on her tail. "Oh no you don't!" he cried, knocking over the furniture as he tried to catch her.

Goldilocks realized she was trapped.

"I'm sorry!" she pleaded. "I was curious—I wanted to see what your funny bear house was like, what your porridge tasted like, and what your chairs and beds were like, too!"

Mr. Bear couldn't believe what he had heard! He moved to give Goldilocks a swipe but missed. She spotted an open window and jumped out of it.

Falling to the ground and landing in a flowerbed she shouted, "Ha! Catch me if you can, old bear!"

Mr. Bear thought he would pop with anger! He raced outside to catch her but alas—she had disappeared into the woods.

Goldilocks returned to her village but no one believed her story. As for the bears, they never left home without locking their door again!

# The Princess and the Pea

by Hans Christian Andersen

# The Princess and the Pea

**M**any years ago, a prince returned home from his travels and informed his mother and father, the king and queen, that he was to be married.

"Oh fantastic, my dear!" said the queen. "Who is the lucky princess?"

"Well," said the prince. "That's the thing. I haven't found her yet. I've spent the last five years exploring the world—but now I am ready to settle down."

"We'll hold a grand ball for you," said the king, "and invite all of the princesses! You'll meet someone you like there!"

The Princess and the Pea

On the evening of the ball, the queen said to her son, "Remember, my young prince, not just any girl will do for you. A true princess is perfectly elegant, softly spoken, and sensitive to the smallest thing."

The prince nodded. "Yes I know, mother," he replied.

The guests started to arrive and one very pretty princess came up to him. Giggling nervously, she asked him to dance. Remembering his mother's advice, the prince decided that a true princess would never laugh so loudly.

"No, thank you," said the prince, politely.

The Princess and the Pea

Soon after, another princess came forward. She was wearing a bright orange dress with black stripes.

"No, thank you," said the prince before she spoke.

"You didn't like her?" asked the king.

"She was dressed like a tiger!" said the prince, appalled.

The evening carried on much like this. One by one the princesses came forward, but the prince always found something he didn't like.

"Look, my boy," said the king. "You need to talk and get to know them."

"Fine …" said the prince in a huff. "I'll dance with … her." He pointed at a princess in a very nice green dress.

"Pleased to meet you," she said kindly.

"Tell me about yourself," he said politely. "What's your name?"

But before she started talking, he spotted that she had mismatched earrings.

"Oh, forget it!" he cried, and he stormed out of the hall.

The next evening the prince was in a bleak mood. "I'll never meet a truly perfect princess," he sighed.

"Patience," said the king with a chuckle. "And perhaps be a bit friendlier."

That made the prince even more miserable. He thought he had been perfectly pleasant.

The Princess and the Pea

All of a sudden there was a sharp knock at the door. Outside, the weather was very stormy—rain was beating against the windowpanes.

"Who could that be?" said the queen.

# The Princess and the Pea

The king himself heaved open the heavy door to the palace. To his great surprise there stood a girl in a cloak, soaking wet from the storm outside.

"I'm sorry to disturb you," she said, "but I've been caught up in the storm and I am far from home."

The girl was drenched! Her dress was covered in mud and her shoes were ruined.

The Princess and the Pea

The king called for a servant to take the girl to get washed and dressed. "Join us when you are ready," he said kindly.

"Who's that?" said the prince when the king returned.

"Just a girl caught in the storm," said the king. "I've asked a servant to take her to one of the spare bedrooms so she can dry off."

The prince was intrigued. "Maybe she'll be a perfect princess," he said to the queen who replied, "Unlikely."

"Hello?" said a soft voice. "May I join you?"

The girl had arrived. She had changed into a woollen dress and was no longer wet. The queen took an instant dislike to her. "She's no princess," she whispered to the prince.

The Princess and the Pea

"Tell me, dear," said the queen haughtily. "Where are you from?"

"I live far away, your majesty over the mountains to the north."

"And why are you so far from home?" asked the king.

"I am exploring," said the girl. "I want to see all corners of the land!"

Now, as you can imagine this interested the prince, who loved adventure himself. The queen, however, did not approve. She wanted her son to see that the girl was vulgar—so that he could continue his search for a perfect princess.

The Princess and the Pea

As the girl spoke, the prince's heart felt light and happy.

"At last!" he thought. "Someone I really like!"

He took his mother to one side to tell her that he thought he had found his bride, but she told him he was wrong. "This girl is hardly quiet or demure." she said to the prince. "And she certainly isn't sensitive to the smallest thing!"

"How can you possibly know that?" said her son.

The queen tried to think of a plan to find out how sensitive the girl was. She thought and thought until she came up with an elaborate idea.

95

**The Princess and the Pea**

So, when no-one was looking, the queen sneaked into the bedroom that the girl would later sleep in. She called three servants to the room at the same time and told them about her plan. The queen ordered them to place three peas from the palace kitchen onto the middle of the girl's bedstead.

"Lay twenty mattresses on top of these peas," she said. "Only someone very sensitive could feel them through all the bedding. If the girl notices, she might just be delicate enough to marry my son."

Later that evening the girl made her way to her bedroom and was surprised to see a very tall bed. It was so high that a ladder had been placed up against it so she could reach the top. She didn't think too much about it, though, as she was so tired. She climbed up and tried to get to sleep. The funny thing was, no matter how much she tried, she couldn't get comfortable. It was as though there were small pebbles in the bed.

The Princess and the Pea

The next morning at breakfast the girl explained that she hadn't slept a wink.

"I scarcely managed to shut my eyes," she said. "There was something terribly uncomfortable in the bed. I have little bruises all over!"

"I'm sorry, my dear," said the king. "I can't imagine how that could be. If you would like to stay longer, we'll move you to a different bedroom."

"Why did you ask her to stay longer?" the queen asked the king, curtly, when they were alone.

"Our son has taken a liking to her …" replied the king with a grin.

The Princess and the Pea

The girl accepted the king's offer to stay longer as she thought that the prince was very good company. They spent the day walking and talking in the palace grounds getting to know each other.

That evening the queen went to the girl's new bedroom with the same servants. She was determined to prove that the girl wasn't delicate. "This time," she said, "place just one pea on the bed and twenty mattresses on top! Let's see if she notices it this that!"

Once again, the girl had a terrible night's sleep. She told them all the next morning that just like on the first night, she had slept awfully and had even more bruises.

"Oh, for goodness' sake!" said the queen. "I give up! I've never met anyone as delicate as you in my life!"

The prince was overjoyed! He asked the girl if she would like to be his wife. The girl was surprised—but very happy. She had fallen in love with the prince and didn't want to leave him.

The queen had no choice but to give her blessing to her son. After all, the girl had passed her tests and had shown that she was as sensitive as a princess!

And so, a grand wedding was planned for one month's time. No expense was spared, and even the peas were included in the big day. They were set neatly into the princess's tiara, which she wore to the ceremony.

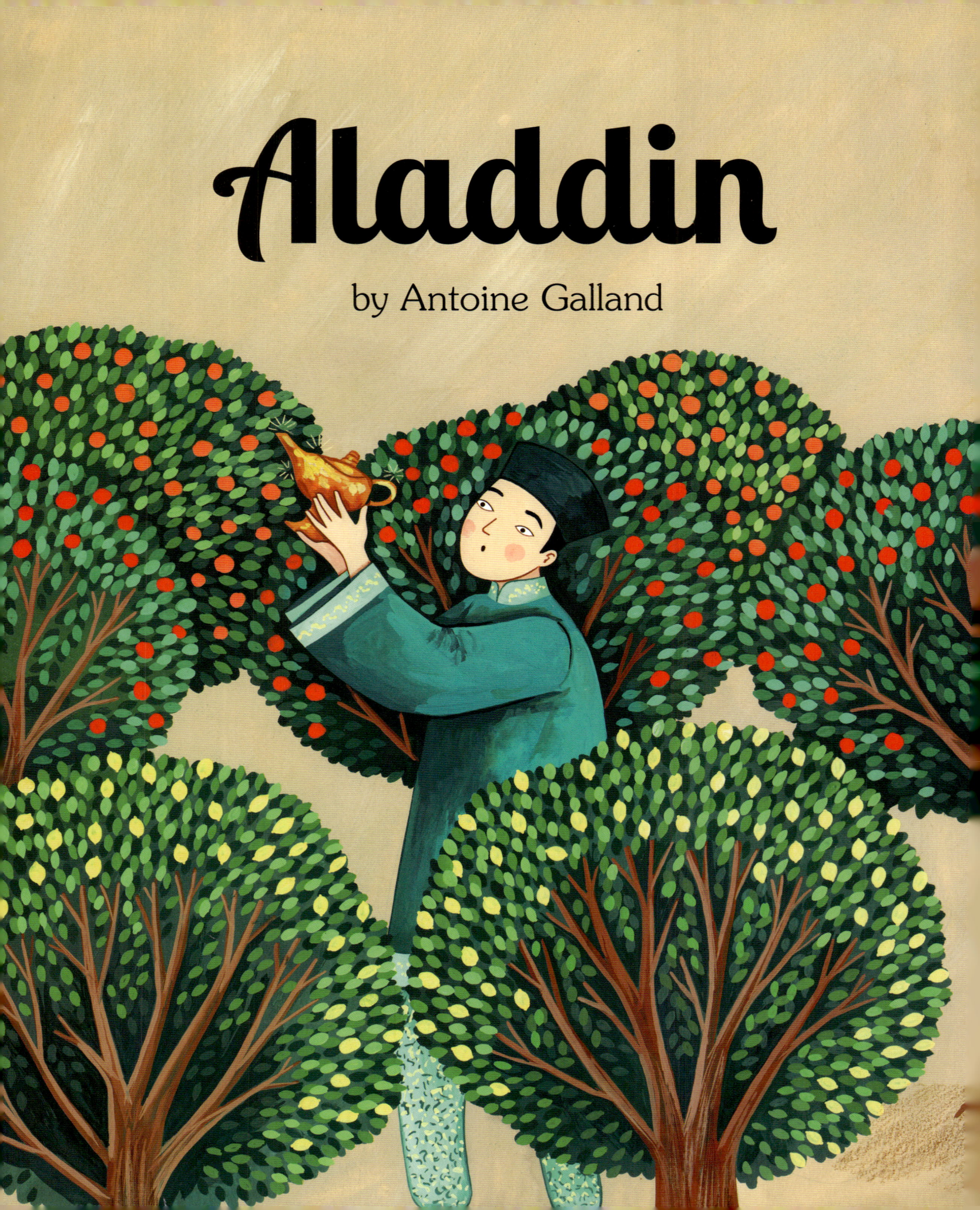

# Aladdin

by Antoine Galland

There once lived a very poor tailor who had a son named Aladdin. The tailor was frustrated because no matter how hard he tried, he could not get his son to work. Instead, Aladdin played in the streets with his lazy friends. The tailor and his wife were nearly at their wits' end about it when, one day, a strange man came to the door of their home. Aladdin thought that this majestic man looked like a magician, but he claimed that he was the tailor's long-lost brother—and Aladdin's uncle.

Aladdin's father was very happy to meet his long-lost brother, but Aladdin was a little suspicious. The man explained how, for the last forty years, he had been roaming the lands searching for his family and now he had found them! He had brought with him baskets of fruit and rice wine, which he offered to Aladdin's mother. She was very pleased with her gifts and asked him to stay for dinner. Over the meal, his new uncle asked Aladdin what he did for work. And of course, Aladdin had no answer.

The uncle said that he would help Aladdin find a trade that he enjoyed, and the next day he took him shopping. He bought the boy a fine suit of clothes before taking him to an empty shop nearby.

"I've bought it for you, Aladdin," said the uncle. "I'll stock it with the most beautiful clothes and you can sell them. You'll make your fortune!"

That evening Aladdin went home to his parents and told them what had happened—and of course they were overjoyed, yet Aladdin felt it was all too good to be true.

A few days later, Aladdin's uncle returned and said he would take Aladdin on a grand trip before he started work.

"We're going far up into the mountains, Aladdin," said his uncle. "I am taking you to find a great treasure that will be all yours."

"Really?" said Aladdin, a little interested. "What is it?"

"You'll soon find out," said his uncle. "Only you are able to touch it, or I would have fetched it for you. You must do exactly what I tell you, or it shall be lost forever."

Aladdin was excited, so he followed his uncle up a long valley between towering mountain tops. They weaved over rocks and cut across many paths until, eventually, they found a sheltered spot where his uncle built a fire.

Aladdin's uncle threw on some kind of scented powder, which crackled and spat in the flames.

"Say the names of your father and grandfather," the uncle ordered Aladdin, who did so.

Immediately a large stone in front of them moved to one side. Where it had laid, there was now a gap. Inside it, Aladdin could see a stone staircase twisting down and out of sight.

"Down you go," said Aladdin's uncle.

"I, I don't want to … " said Aladdin.

To his surprise, his uncle stood up and grabbed Aladdin's jacket. "You will do as I say," he growled. "Go down the stairs and through the great hall. Do not touch a thing or you will die. At the end of the hall is a garden with many fruit trees. Walk to the terrace in the middle of the trees and find the oil lamp. Bring it to me."

Aladdin felt quite scared—his uncle was behaving differently. He thought about running away, but he didn't know the way back through the mountains.

"OK … " Aladdin trembled.

He stepped onto the staircase and walked down. It was exactly as his uncle had described. Aladdin ran through the hall and the orchard to the lamp and dashed back again as quickly as he could. Once he was back above ground, his uncle asked politely for the lamp, but Aladdin no longer trusted him.

"I'll give it to you when we get home," he said tentatively.

This made his uncle furious! "Give it to me now!" he cried.

"You said it is mine, Uncle," said Aladdin.

"I'm not your uncle, you fool!" the man shouted. "I'm a magician, and I'm banished from the world below. I needed someone—anyone—to get the lamp for me! I only pretended to be your uncle to get you here!"

All of a sudden there was a loud crack of thunder—a storm was moving in. The noise distracted the magician, giving Aladdin a chance to run and hide behind a large rock. The man was so frustrated that he stormed off, cursing the day he chose Aladdin as his helper.

So Aladdin was safe—but lost in the mountains with no way to get home. He sat in fear while holding onto the lamp. As he wondered what to do, he noticed that the lamp was very dirty and began polishing it with the corner of his jacket.

All of a sudden a great big genie appeared in front of him. "You summoned me?" it bellowed. "What is your wish? I shall grant it."

Aladdin was overwhelmed! "Take me home!" he squeaked.

"It is done!" said the genie, and before he could blink, Aladdin was standing at the front door of his house.

Aladdin

Once the surprise of having a magic lamp and a genie that granted wishes had sunk in, Aladdin began wondering what he could do with his new power. He thought about the beautiful princess, who was about to be married to a prince from a far-off land. It was said that she wasn't happy about the match.

"I would like to marry her instead," Aladdin said to his mother.

"You'll need to make a very grand gesture indeed for that," she smiled.

Aladdin thought for a minute and then rubbed his lamp again.

"Genie!" he cried. "Build me a palace made of the finest marble. Decorate it with precious gemstones and paint the walls with gold. All of the carpets are to be made from the softest velvet. I want the rooms to be filled with diamonds and rubies for the princess!"

And so the genie did as he was asked. Aladdin sent a message to the king to say that he wished to marry the princess instead—would they come and see his palace in all its glory?

Well, when the king saw the palace he was convinced that Aladdin would make a much better husband for his daughter, and luckily the princess liked Aladdin very much.

They were married shortly after, and they led a very happy life—Aladdin provided his new wife and the people of the land with whatever they needed, thanks to the magic lamp and the wish-granting genie.

But far away in the mountains, the magician heard of Aladdin's success and felt robbed. He decided to put an end to Aladdin's good fortunes.

The magician returned to Aladdin's home and took with him a beautiful new lamp, just like Aladdin's, but shinier. He offered it to the princess in return for any old lamps that she happened to have lying around. She happily swapped it, because she didn't know that the lamp was magic.

The magician left the palace, laughing to himself, and as soon as he was out of sight, rubbed the lamp to make the genie appear.

"What is your wish?" said the genie.

"I wish you to take Aladdin's palace and his princess to the jungle."

And so, as nothing was out of the genie's power, he granted the wish.

When Aladdin returned and found his home and bride gone, he knew who had done it. He told the king that he would find the magician and rescue his daughter.

The journey was long and treacherous, taking many months.

Eventually, when he found the dwelling, he saw his princess in the distance. She was sitting with the magician on a beautiful balcony. The poor princess looked very sullen.

Aladdin crept up to the palace and when the princess saw him, placed his finger over his lips. The princess began talking to the magician to distract him while Aladdin climbed through one of the palace's large ornate windows.

The lamp was tied to the magician's belt, which was draped over his bed. Aladdin grabbed it and rubbed the lamp, just like always, and made his wish—to return home with the palace and the princess and for the magician to disappear at last.

Aladdin's wish came true. He was reunited with his princess, and together they lived happily ever after.

# Thumbelina

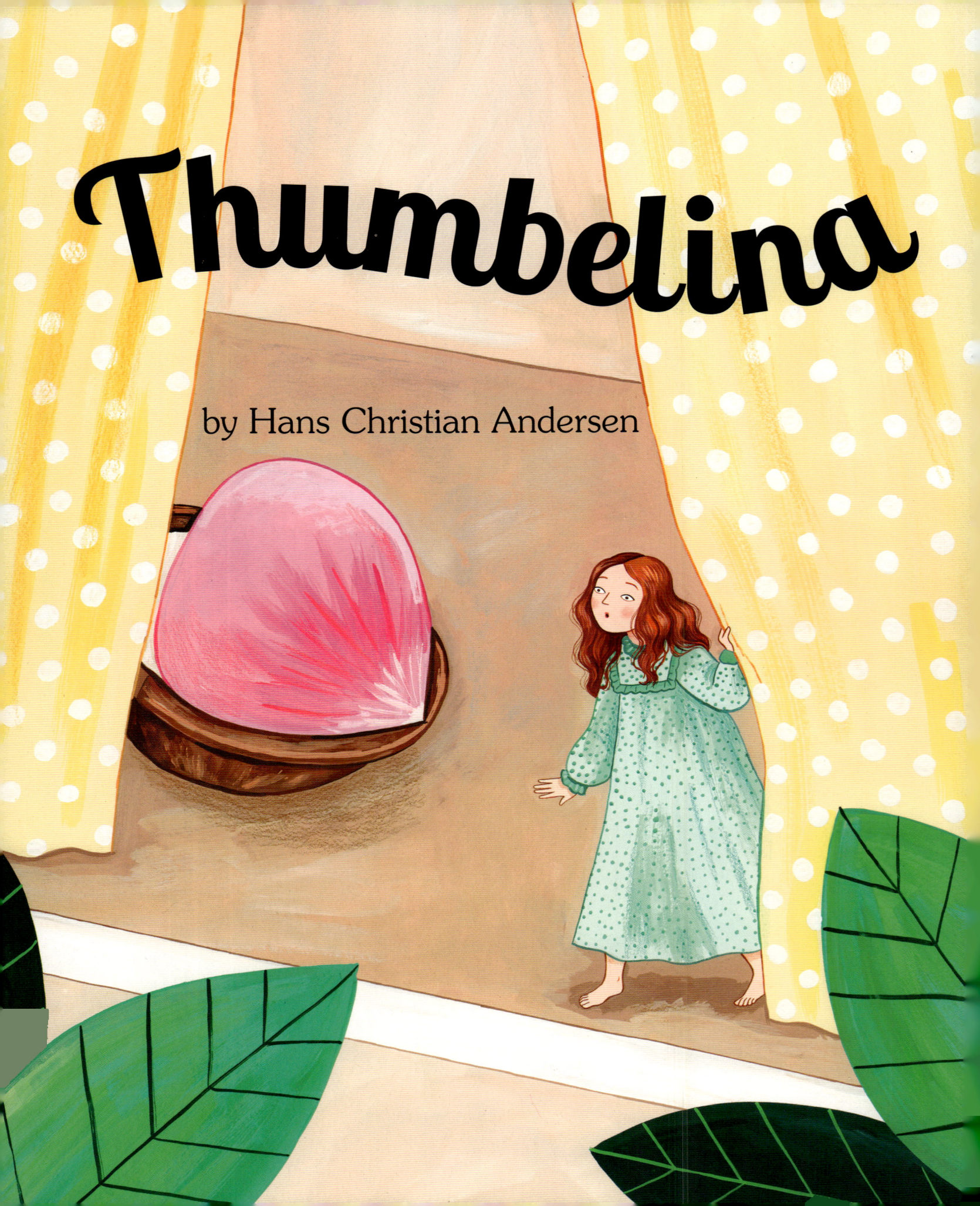

by Hans Christian Andersen

Thumbelina

There once was a peasant woman who had lived a very good life but had never had a baby. She had a beautiful garden of flowers that she tended carefully, but she found herself lonely and longed for a child.

One day, she decided to visit a witch who she had heard could help her. She made the long journey to the witch's house in the woods. Right away, the witch saw how the woman yearned for a child and the sadness it was causing her not to have one. So, she decided to grant her wish.

# Thumbelina

"I will help you," she croaked. "Take this barleycorn and plant it in a pot. Tend to it carefully and the child you long for will be yours."

The woman didn't understand, but she took the barleycorn, thanked the witch, and went home.

When she got back, she planted the barleycorn in a pot on the windowsill. She faithfully cared for it every day, even though she couldn't see how it could make her dream come true.

Eventually, the barleycorn sprouted. First it grew a shoot, then a pretty little flower bud appeared.

Thumbelina

Then, one day the flower bud opened to reveal a tiny girl inside! The peasant woman loved the girl as soon as she saw her. She was no bigger than the woman's thumb, so she called her Thumbelina.

Thumbelina grew up knowing that she was a miracle. She loved her mother very much, and she loved her home on the windowsill.

"The big wide world isn't safe for a girl as small as you," said Thumbelina's mother. "But at least you can watch it from here."

And she did watch it, until one night a shadowy figure crept through the slightly open window. The sleeping Thumbelina was jolted awake as she was snatched up and carried away—by a large toad!

"She will make an excellent bride for my son," crooned the toad as he lolloped back toward the cool, shady riverbank where he lived. Thumbelina was terrified.

"Please put me down!" she cried.

"Shan't," snapped the toad. "You will be my son's wife."

He carried Thumbelina to the river and placed her on a lily pad that was floating in the middle of the running water.

Thumbelina

"Son!" the toad called. "I have found you a bride."
A large brown toad with many warts crawled out of the reeds. Thumbelina was disgusted.
"Let me go!" she cried.
But they would not. Poor Thumbelina cried and cried. Two goldfish swimming below heard her weeping.
"Let's help her," one said, and together they chewed through the stalk that was tethering the lily pad.

Thumbelina drifted far down the river. Eventually, she drifted to the riverbank and stepped onto dry land. She found herself in a woodland surrounded by trees that looked enormous to her. Thumbelina didn't know how to find her way home—and she was very cold. Winter was coming and she shivered in the frosty air. As Thumbelina wandered aimlessly, snow began to fall. She searched for shelter till she came across a small hole in a tree. Inside it, a little mouse was bustling around.

"What are you doing outside?" the mouse cried. "Come in, my dear! I'm Mrs. Mouse."

"Thank you," said Thumbelina. "I'm Thumbelina. I am lost and very far from home."

"Well then, you must stay until the snow passes," said Mrs. Mouse, leading her into a warm and snug underground nest. "I've got enough food to last us until the spring."

Thumbelina was touched by her kindness. Mrs. Mouse fed her, gave her a bed, and even made her new clothes.

# Thumbelina

The snow lasted for weeks and weeks. Thumbelina felt lucky to have found such a kind friend.

One day, Mrs. Mouse was whisking around the nest cleaning and tidying everything.

"What's the occasion?" asked Thumbelina curiously.

"The mole is coming to visit!" Mrs. Mouse squeaked. "He is blind, of course, but I wish to impress him for your sake. He needs a wife to help him and, since he is very rich, he would be a fine match for you."

Thumbelina didn't like the sound of that, as she thought back to the awful toad who had wanted to marry her.

"I don't think I want to get married," she told Mrs. Mouse.

"Oh, don't be silly," Mrs. Mouse flapped her paws. "You need to marry well if you are to live comfortably. I'm only thinking of you, my dear."

Thumbelina knew Mrs. Mouse was trying to be good to her, and she had already been so kind that Thumbelina couldn't bear to disappoint her. So, she went along with the cleaning and resolved to be as polite as possible to the mole when he arrived.

When Mr. Mole lumbered into the nest, bumping into the walls, Thumbelina struggled to suppress a shudder.

He was old but more than that, he was grumpy and rude. Thumbelina didn't care for him at all, but Mrs. Mouse made her sing for him, and the mole instantly fell in love.

He invited Thumbelina to visit his home. Not knowing how to refuse, she went. It was grand indeed with many large tunnels and chambers. But it was also cold.

In the middle of one of the passages lay a swallow. The mole nudged it grumpily as he went past.

"This bird came and died in the middle of my tunnel, so now I'm stuck with it," he said without feeling.

Thumbelina was saddened that the poor bird had died, and nobody cared about it. When she went back to Mrs. Mouse's that night, the bird was all that she could think of and she thought that the least she could do was cover it up. She grabbed a quilt and crept back to the mole's tunnels.

Laying the quilt over the swallow, she gave it a hug and whispered, "I care about you."

Just then, she felt the bird's heart thump in its chest.

# Thumbelina

The next moment, it fluttered its wings and got to its feet.

"Thank you for helping me," the swallow cheeped. "I thought I would freeze in these tunnels!"

He hopped away and flew out toward the sky.

Thumbelina was happy to have helped the bird, but she had started to feel trapped herself.

The mole announced the next day that he wanted to marry her.

"Mrs. Mouse, you have been so kind to me," said Thumbelina. "But I cannot marry the mole. I do not care for him."

"Nonsense! Think of the riches you will have," sang Mrs. Mouse as she merrily sewed a wedding dress.

On the day of the wedding, Thumbelina could barely hold back her tears. As she walked to the ceremony, she ducked behind a tree to sob. Then, she heard a rustle and there standing next to her was the swallow she had helped!

Thumbelina

"Do you wish to escape? Then come with me!" the swallow called, lowering his body down so that Thumbelina could climb onto his back.

"Thank you!" Thumbelina cried.

The swallow flew her to a field of beautiful flowers. She asked the swallow to set her down there. He did as she asked and they said good-bye.

Thumbelina had just sat down in the cradle of a bright pink flower when a handsome fairy stepped into view. She had never seen anyone as small as herself before and she was enchanted. He introduced himself as the Fairy Prince and asked if he could show her his kingdom.

Thumbelina went with him and met many other fairies, who all lived in the beautiful bright blooms.

After many weeks, the Fairy Prince asked Thumbelina to be his wife. She had fallen deeply in love with him and gladly accepted his proposal.

Thumbelina

The Fairy Prince gave Thumbelina a pair of wings as a wedding gift, and together they lived happily as Prince and Princess in the fairy flower meadow.

At night, Thumbelina would sing the fairy kingdom to sleep with the same song that she used to sing to her mother. All the birds heard it too and learned it.

Back in her cottage, Thumbelina's mother heard the birds' song and knew her girl was safe out in the big wide world. At last she went to sleep with happiness in her heart.

# About the Stories

About the Stories

# Cinderella

There are numerous different versions of the Cinderella fairy tale from all over the world. Often, the heroine is cast from her home and has to prove herself in some way in order to return to her original social standing. A Cinderella tale usually rewards characters that are good, clever, and graceful—such as the heroine herself. If a character doesn't act fairly, however, they often find themselves worse off than they were at the beginning. In some versions, the stepsisters are forced to work in the palace kitchen, while in others they are never seen again!

About the Stories

# Puss in Boots

Originally called The Master Cat, Puss in Boots was published by Perrault in the late 1600s. In this rags-to-riches tale, Puss is a classic trickster. He uses his quick wit and intelligence to convince people to do what he wants through cunning, risk-taking, and even telling lies. How else would a cat convince an ogre to turn into a mouse? The cat's master, the "Marquis of Carabas", is a strange character, as he himself does very little to alter the course of his life, yet circumstances dramatically change for the better because of Puss.

About the Stories

# Little Red Riding Hood

Little Red Riding Hood is perhaps one of the best-known fairy tales. This story was told all over Europe and belongs to the folk tradition of spoken storytelling. Charles Perrault, a French author, was the first person to publish it at the end of the 17th century. Since then, the tale has been told many times, so there are lots of different versions—including one where Little Red Riding Hood isn't so lucky, and the wolf gets his meal at the end! The tale is cautionary—warning children that there may be dangers in the world, and that part of growing up is learning to be a good judge of another's character.

About the Stories

# Snow White

First published by the Brothers Grimm, this moral tale is centuries old. Snow White's good and kind nature shows us that beauty comes from within, while the actions of the stepmother teach us the dangers of vanity and jealousy. Some historians believe that the character of Snow White was based on a German countess named Margaretha von Waldeck. She was sent away by her stepmother before falling in love with a prince, who later became the king of Spain. We don't know if this is true, of course, but it does make us wonder if there are sometimes elements of truth in fairy tales.

About the Stories

# The Three Bears

In the original version of The Three Bears, there was no Goldilocks—instead an old woman broke into the three bears' house. It was in the early 1900s that the character of the intruder became the one we know today—the mischievous, golden-haired girl. Goldilocks is very selfish and disruptive in the tale. The story provides a moral lesson to children teaching them to respect the property and belongings of others.

About the Stories

# The Princess and the Pea

Hans Christian Andersen wrote the short tale, The Princess and the Pea, to make the case that sensitivity is the most important quality of all in someone born to rule. Unlike many other fairy tale characters, the princess doesn't have to go on a quest or do anything to prove herself—instead, her delicate nature is quite enough to show that she could be a royal. There are other tales that have a similar theme, showing that this idea might have been popular at the time. It was originally published in the 1830s in *Tales, Told for Children, First Collection*.

About the Stories

# Aladdin

The story of Aladdin was included in a translated collection of Middle Eastern tales called *The Arabian Nights,* or *One Thousand and One Nights* in the early 1700s. In this version, Aladdin lives in a city in China and so early illustrations show him as Chinese. It was only in the 20th century, when Aladdin was made popular by a cartoon movie, that it became common to depict him as being from the Middle East instead.

About the Stories

# Thumbelina

Thumbelina is one of Danish author Hans Christian Andersen's earliest tales. It was originally called Tommelise and tells the tale of a very sweet—and very small—girl who falls in love with a fairy prince but not before she escapes the unwanted attention of some other admirers, including a toad! This tale shows us that staying positive is very important. Thumbelina stays honest and kind throughout all of her difficulties, and her tale ends happily.

# Quick Quiz

1. How many stepsisters does Cinderella have?
2. What is Puss' favourite item of clothing?
3. Who is Little Red Riding Hood on her way to visit?
4. Goldilocks wears a red cloak. True or false?
5. Does the queen in Snow White look at her reflection in a lake or a mirror?
6. In one of the tales, a girl proves that she has the sensitivity of a true princess by sleeping on what vegetable?
7. Which magical object does the genie come out from in Aladdin?
8. Which animal kidnaps Thumbelina from the windowsill?

**Answers:** 1. Two. 2. His boots. 3. Her grandmother. 4. False—Little Red Riding Hood wears a red cloak. 5. A mirror. 6. Peas. 7. A lamp. 8. A toad.

# About the Illustrator and Author

## Helena Pérez García

Award-winning Spanish artist Helena Pérez García illustrates books for both children and adults internationally. Her work is inspired by the flowers and trees of nature and walks in the parks of Madrid where she lives. Helena's unique style is achieved through water-based paint and pencil on paper.

## Claire Philip

Claire Philip is an experienced children's author and editor based in the beautiful Lake District in the UK. She loves writing both fact and fiction books for young children—especially magical fairy tales. As well as working on books, she enjoys walking in the hills, yoga, and cuddling her cat Bruce.